TAKEN BY MY TBR

Holly Wilde

Copyright © 2024 Holly Wilde

All rights reserved

The characters and events portrayed in this book are fictitious. Any similarity to real persons, living or dead, is coincidental and not intended by the author.

No part of this book may be reproduced, or stored in a retrieval system, or transmitted in any form or by any means, electronic, mechanical, photocopying, recording, or otherwise, without express written permission of the publisher.

ISBN: 9798326647542
Imprint: Independently published

Cover design by: Holly Wilde
Printed in the United States of America

"Just one more book" really means "Just one more fictional crush." My dear reader, you deserve a world brimming with characters brought to life.

CONTENTS

Title Page
Copyright
Dedication
Taken by my TBR
Content Warnings
Chapter One — 1
Chapter Two — 5
Chapter Three — 9
Chapter Four — 12
Chapter Five — 15
Chapter Six — 17
Chapter Seven — 20
Chapter Eight — 26
Chapter Nine — 30
Chapter Ten — 42
Epilogue — 46
Coming soon — 49
About The Author — 51
Books By This Author — 53
THE END — 55

TAKEN BY MY TBR

Tossing and turning doesn't just apply to a restless night in bed. It also is what happens when you can't find a book to quench your mood-reader thirst. Turning pages and tossing books into the growing TBR stack is how Paige spends her night. Unfortunately for her, giving up on her night of reading isn't an option.

When her stack of books comes to life, they make their intention clear: tonight is the night the TBR gets its finish. The only question is, will the happy ending lead to a happily ever after?

CONTENT WARNINGS

This story is a compilation of many popular genres in the literary and romance world. As a result, it includes certain tropes and themes that may not suit all readers. Please review the following list to ensure that nothing in the plot will make you feel uncomfortable or trigger any emotions you do not wish to experience.

Death of a Parent
Death of a Friend
Murder
Kidnapping
Dubious Consent
Weapon Play
Blood
Gore (not graphic, but hinted at)
Thoughts of Suicide
Love Triangle
Self Harm
Light Bondage and Torture
CNC
Degredation

Please know there is no HEA in this book, even though there is a happy ending.

CHAPTER ONE

"Oh, I bought this one last month when it came out." Lindsey, the bookstore clerk, says while she tucks the receipt neatly behind the cover of the latest bestseller I'm buying. Admiring the gilded edges and how they contrast with the amethyst artwork, I'm thrilled to finally hold this story in my hands.

"How did you like it?"

The hype surrounding this book has been nonstop since the publication date was released. Considering I missed my chance to get a copy the moment it came out, I'm letting myself splurge on the special edition I found on display.

"Well, it ended up in the TBR," she says with a shrug, "You know how it goes."

The ever growing TBR pile is a dirty little secret all readers share. "I absolutely know what you mean. Half of my shelves are storage for books I've bought, but haven't cracked open. I was going to start one of them today, but decided to come here instead. Now I have this beauty to keep me company tonight."

"I think I'll start reading this tonight, too. In fact, Paige, you can hold me to it. The next time you pop in, ask me about my progress!"

Some people have a local cafe they frequent, I have my local bookstore. Not only do they know my name, but they share my love for all things fantasy and romance. It's fun knowing a store full of people who can recommend a book that will make me blush and gush. That's why I'm smitten with this place, and I consider my growing TBR to be a staple of keeping the community book hub alive.

"That sounds amazing, Linds. I'll see you next time!" Waving my book in the air to say goodbye, I leave the shop and start my walk back home. Being only two blocks away from my apartment, I rarely find an excuse to keep myself from browsing for just a bit. Which inevitably turns into a book buying binge. Still, one more never hurt anybody.

Living nearby means that even when work keeps me busy, it's never a problem to quickly grab what I need and leave without taking up too much time. Which is exactly what happened today. I've been assigned to a high-maintenance client who's been a persistent thorn in my side for the past two months. Today was finally the last day for me to handle the assignment, and I couldn't be happier. Trading my lunch for an extra coffee, I worked right up to the last minute, fixing and finalizing every request until just after six. With a strong need to celebrate my freetime returning, and the shop closing in under an hour, I grabbed a bagel and raced over to get the book I've been eyeing for so long. Heading back home with the novel in my hands, I swear I can hear the siren song of my comfy chair floating through the neighborhood as I get closer to my apartment.

Rummaging in my bag to find my keys, I take the steps two at a time to get to my front door. As if they can sense my joy, work calls. Though I have a strong urge to ignore them, I know I can't. Especially if I want to keep buying necessities like food. And books. I turn the key and open the door while I answer the call.

"Paige speaking."

"Oh, good! You picked up. Look, Paige. The client sent back some revisions and we need you to look over their notes and fix everything before nine." Glancing at the clock on the microwave, I stifle a groan when I see that it's already after seven. Are they really expecting me to cram what is surely a minimum of five hours worth of work into only two?

"Yeah, of course I can do that. I'll get right on it." My professional tone hides the disappointment mounting within.

"You're one in a million, I knew I could count on you to get this done. Feel free to reach out if there's anything you need." My boss hangs up on me before I can reply, but it's not like he needs to hear anything else from me. I've already told him what he wanted, that I'm ready to sit down and suffer through the grind for the rest of my evening.

Reluctantly heading to my bedroom, I scan my perfectly curated bookshelves to see if there's a spot for my latest addition. Seeing no space right away, and sensing the invisible tug of my client through the computer, I set the novel on top of the cream upholstered chair in the corner of my room. My fingers refuse to leave the cover of the book even though I've put it down. It's like I'm mourning the night of relaxation that's so long overdue. I should be here with my bum in the seat, a blanket tucked around my shoulders like a cape, tea steaming beside me, and mind lost in a far away realm where deadlines and edits don't exist.

A crash of thunder overhead makes me jump, effectively prying my fingers from the memory of what could be as I hop away from the book in fright. Just great. A storm is all I need to remind me that I can't curl up in a big comfy ball with the rain pounding in the background. Instead, I'll be pounding the keys, steadily clicking my fingers on the computer. With a sigh, I begrudgingly shuffle over to my closet. If I'm forced to work after hours, then I'll do it in pajamas and fuzzy socks. It's the only form of rebellion I have. Stripping down to my undies, I look for something that is, what I like to call, at-home business casual. Grabbing the oversized tie-dyed pastel sweatshirt as well as some over the knee pale blue fuzzy socks, I slip them on and trudge over to my desk. Opening my email before I sit down, I skim the contents to figure out what kind of night it's going to be. My heart sinks when I see note after note of revisions and requests. I drag myself to the kitchen for a bowl of pretzels and a soda, this night calls for reinforcements of the sugar variety. Tossing a few mini chocolate chips into the bowl with my snack, I go back and set up camp at my desk with the hope that I can get out of this night with enough energy to read before I pass out.

CHAPTER TWO

After sitting for three hours at my desk, tucking myself under my blankets should be a welcome relief. The new book may be in my lap, but my good mood that came from the thrill of purchasing it is long gone. All I have is my exhaustion and my stubborn determination to read at least one chapter before my eyes decide that they can't stay open any longer. Sitting on my bed, staring at the cover, I will myself to crack the spine and just start the first sentence.

❋ ❋ ❋

"Curse whoever thought that bringing needlework to the briar was a good idea on today of all days." I instantly regret speaking the words. Because I know who packed the embroidery, and it's wrong to curse the dead.

Considering I don't know where the warriors are, I should keep moving. I need to seek shelter, but I can't stop myself from glancing back. Scanning the foot of the hill yields nothing. The brambles are too thick to see Lucandra's body, but I can picture the way it's sprawled on the ground where I left her. Poor Luci. None but she could handle being assigned to the Princess of Mora with the same tenacity and resilience. While my parents raised the walls to protect us from invasion, she raised me.

I suddenly feel like a child again. No matter that I turned nineteen only yesterday, I feel small and alone. If I let myself be honest, I feel frightened in a way that only a child knows. It's a consuming fear, believing there is nothing I can do to help myself. My only choice is to wait until someone bigger, someone more than me, comes around to save the day. However, I am not a child. There is no one in this country that will come and save me. I am alone, and I shall have to save myself.

Grabbing my skirts, I yet again find my voice wanting to curse my maiden. This time for dressing me in the most impractical clothing for climbing hills. Though, I am certain she didn't suspect that the Naeyle Warriors would swoop in and make good on their declaration of destruction.

I can still hear her voice as she brushed out my curls this morning. "You should wear the red, it's your father's favorite. And from what I hear, today is a good day to be in his favor."

Perhaps we should have thought a moment about why my father was in a foul mood. Instead, I allowed her to put on one of the most complicated dresses in my wardrobe. All for the sake of appearing more regal, more dainty, more like the charming little daughter I am expected to be. I didn't even see him this morning, so it was all for naught.

My heart tightens in my chest, the emotions gripping stronger than my fists clutching my gown. Realization dawns that I may never see my family again. My feet fumble beneath me and I lose the will to keep upright. Tears stream down my face as I kneel on the mossy ground, my skirts pooled around like a sea of blood. The red fabric spreading in all directions paints the picture of my heartache seeping from a wound, yet there's no simple flesh for me to mend.

"My Lady."

A deep voice startles me from my mourning. Curses flood my mind as I realize the foolishness of sitting like a target, clad in the brightest color on the highest ground during a dragon attack. I keep my head bowed low, hoping to buy time by concealing my face.

"My Lady," he repeats, drawing nearer. The tips of his scuffed boots come into view, their soles caked with dried mud. Like creeping vines, tendrils of shadows trail down in front of him, reaching out for me. One brushes back my hair with its inky heat, lifting my chin so I'm forced to meet his gaze. There's no mistaking him for anything but a dragon rider. His attire, the color of a moonless night, matches the hue of his hair. I imagine his soul is equally obsidian if he can command darkness with such expertise.

"Are you alone?" His eyes, the liquid pools of gold, look around quickly for any signs of ambush.

"You're here, aren't you? That would mean I'm not alone." My glare doesn't feel as strong as I'd like, especially when he merely smiles down at me.

"I suppose we're together now. Come, it's time to get up. You're not safe here." The shadow releases my chin and reaches for my hand, urging me to rise.

"Why should I believe I'm safe with you? I'd rather stay here, thank you very much." But the shadow tugs harder until I'm forced to my feet.

"I never said you were safe with me," he replies, turning away. "I only said you weren't safe here." His sword, streaked with rust, catches my attention as the shadows pull me closer. Chills slither down my spine when I get close enough to see that I'm mistaken. The rust is blood. He notices my shudder and turns back to me.

"Are you cold, My Lady?"

"I'm not your lady. And I'm not cold," I assert. When his eyebrows rise, prompting me to continue, I add, "You have blood on your blade."

"Oh, yes. That. Unfortunately, the blood belongs to your King." The shock evident on my face has nothing to do with the magnificent beast flying towards us. Its scales are as richly red as my dress, and as terrifying as the blood of my father splattered across the steel.

As the color drains from my face, I stagger, feeling the ground shift beneath me. Swiftly, the shadowy embrace gives way to the stranger's arms, enfolding me protectively before I can faint. My eyes meet the glint of the sword's hilt, poised ominously over his shoulder, and I fight the urge to recoil. My heart races with a wild rhythm, and I hate the steady beat echoing back at me from his chest. Despite the turmoil swirling within, I manage to hold back my sobs.

Sensing my distress, he leans in close, his breath warm and sweet against my ear. "I swear to you, My Lady, so long as you do not cross me, this blade shall never be turned against you," *he murmurs soothingly. The ache in my core yearns to believe him, even if my mind clamors for vengeance.*

CHAPTER THREE

"Sorry, shadow daddy."

I'm sure the tale in my lap is as epic as everyone says, but I'm not in the mood for big drama right now. Life is dramatic enough. Still, I'm stubborn and want to keep reading. I just don't know what I'm in the mood for.

Leaving the comfort of my bed is hard, but necessary. Setting the book on the corner chair, I turn my attention to my TBR. Opting to go for one that's half finished, I select a dark romance with all the common tropes. It's a forced marriage where the characters have to stay together for some alliance. I remember some of the story, but not a lot. Vague details about a woman's parents sending her to the altar with a rich, darkly handsome man swirl around in my mind. Maybe a good sex scene will break me out of my funk.

"It's worth a try," I say to no one in particular as I make my way back to bed. Once I'm settled and cozy, I thumb through the pages to find the dagger-shaped bookmark and let myself get lost in the story.

❋ ❋ ❋

His aqua flecked eyes are the coldest blue as he stares at me harder than the steel pressing into my throat.

"Did you really think that you could have dinner here without me finding out about it?"

It's a rhetorical question, and I know that he doesn't expect me to answer. Even if I tried, the bobbing of my throat would just end up digging the knife into my neck. He plays dangerously, and someone should teach him that even he can't win all the games. For the briefest moment, I'm tempted to be the one to ruin him. But if I let him kill me here, then I wouldn't witness his downfall. And that means I'd miss watching the carefully stacked tower of authority and power crumble and fall around him.

The scratch of the knife's tip drags up to my lips, not deep enough to cut, but I wouldn't be surprised to find a faint line of pink left in its path.

"Open."

He knows I won't obey. Yet he looks at the way the metal indents my plump skin like he wants to feel it between us as we kiss. The sight of my red lipstick on the blade excites him to the point that he wishes he would draw blood. I keep my back rigid against the wall behind me and wait for him to make his next move. Flexing his wrist, he brings his hand down to the crown of my head, swirling the pads of his fingers gently with the intention of mussing the strands in order to get a good grip.

"Fuck, you're so beautiful," the words come out hoarse and breathless. Leaning down to speak into my ear, he says, "I bet Shiloh thought he was a lucky fucking guy sitting across from you. Too bad he didn't know you belong to me."

Poor Shiloh. I close my eyes to hide any trace of emotion from my face. Not that I really feel anything for my coworker, but he's nice and he's different. Different from the man I was forced to marry. So when he asked me to dinner, I didn't see a reason to say no. Afterall, we were the last to leave the office and I was hungry. I certainly didn't think that my husband, in name only, would even notice.

Forgetting the knife at my mouth, the words rush from me. "Don't hurt him. He doesn't know I'm married."

He's so close to me that his growl rumbles through my belly as *he says, "That's a mistake you shouldn't have made."*

Fingers roughly grip my chin before his lips crash against mine. The tang of copper overwhelms me as his tongue pushes past the knife and into my mouth. He's cut himself while claiming me, the knife opening his tongue as he licks away my concerns. It's like he is giving me the blood as an offering. It's possessive, passionate, and reckless the way he kisses me. For a moment, I almost think he loves me. But then his hands reach down and crawl up my skirt, and I'm reminded that this is just his game. He couldn't love someone to save his own life, he just wants to make a point that I belong to him. By fucking me in the restaurant while his men watch the corridor entrance, he's driving home the fact that he owns this city. And that he owns me.

The knife once poised between us is now angled against my panties. It slices a hole along my slit and I whimper into his mouth from the sensation of the tip gliding across my sensitive flesh.

CHAPTER FOUR

Usually, knives pressed between thighs give me butterflies, but tonight the only things fluttering are my eyelids. Stacking the dark romance on top of the fantasy novel sitting in the chair, I set my sights back on my TBR. The blurbs begin to blur while I browse. I'm about to give up when a sea green spine catches my attention. Water droplets and bubbles splattered around the cover discreetly hint at the seamonster romance between the pages. The patter of rain on my window mirrors the book I'm holding, and I tuck myself under the blankets as another storm rolls through.

* * *

"Come with me."

I nearly drop my fork when his voice slices through my mind. Steadying my grip, I try to reorient myself with the conversations happening around me.

The sensation of telepathy tingles through me once more, urging me with his insistent command. "Come with me,"

"I can't leave right now," I reply. Telepathy is still new to me, and it feels strange using it as a form of communication. Especially when I'm in a room full of people who wouldn't understand that the currents of fate have intertwined my destiny with that of a merman's.

"You belong with me."

Prior to yesterday, marrying Brad was the only thing on my mind. Then I was tossed overboard during a sailing excursion, only a mere two days before our wedding. My body isn't the only thing that plunged into the waters. My heart fell deeply as well the moment I was saved by Caspian. He isn't wrong, in some strange and unexplainable way, I do belong to him.

"We have rules here, and running into the ocean is one of those things that wouldn't be okay to do," I say. It's the only answer I can give. How am I to tell this creature about things like manners and propriety?

"Your laws forbid you to step foot into the ocean just because the moon is risen?"

"No, it's not the law. It's just known that the ocean isn't a place to visit. Especially for a woman alone, and even more so at night." My in-mind conversation is interrupted when a hand is placed gently upon my shoulder.

"Are you doing okay, darling?" Brad's brow is furrowed with concern, and I realize I've held my fork hovered beside my mouth this entire time I was talking telepathically.

Setting my fork on my plate, I bring my napkin to my mouth and dab the corners gently. "You know," I say to my fiance, "I am feeling a bit off. I think I'll step out for some fresh air." Nodding politely at the guests sitting around me, I excuse myself from the table.

Brad scoots his chair back, preparing to assist me until I hurriedly add, "No need to leave the festivities. I'll be gone for only a moment. Please, enjoy the food." He gives me a look of uncertainty before placing his napkin back in his lap and returning to the conversation. Maybe my merman is right, maybe it isn't that hard to follow your heart. Because right now, my heart is tugging me into the sea.

The chill of the sand bites at my feet as I step onto the shore. Honestly, it feels refreshing after being constrained in strappy heels. I glance back at the house to make sure no one has seen me. The noise from conversations and elegant music float down through the open windows. I can make out the silhouettes of my guests and a part of me *aches to be happy with them, like I used to be.*

Turning towards the sea, I whisper, "Are you there?"

"You came," his voice echoes in my mind, drawing me closer to the edge where the waves meet the shore. The icy touch of the surf caresses my ankles, sending shivers down my spine.

Panic flares within me as I call out, "Where are you?"

"Who are you talking to?" Brad's voice pierces the stillness, startling me so much that I stumble. Yet again, I find myself plunging into the sea. His hand reaches out to pull me up, but something beneath the surface coils around me.

"You're here," echoes the voice in my mind.

Terrified by what he's seeing, Brad shouts, "Oh my God, Jemma! Grab onto me."

Tentacles wrap around me, their touch both foreign and familiar. Guiding me with gentle insistence, they drag me deeper. Brad's frantic shouts fade into the distance, but his grip on my arm is steadfast. With both men holding me tightly, I realize that I am literally torn between two loves, each vying for my heart. But I only have one heart to give.

CHAPTER FIVE

When well written, a love triangle can rip your heart apart in time with the lead characters. Clearly, I'm just not in the mood to have my heart, or my panties, torn to shreds. Looks like I'm on strike three, but I refuse to be out. Adding tentacle man to the growing stack on my chair, I face the shelves once again. This time, I'm going to leave it up to chance. Putting a finger on one of the spines, I close my eyes and run my hand back and forth over the books. Dipping and rising, the different widths undulate beneath my touch. They jump to the beat of the rain on my window, yearning for their moment in the spotlight.

Lightning flashes so brightly that the glare pierces through my closed lids. Taking the thunder as my cue to stop, I grasp the book and slide it from its home. One glance at the eerie cover is all it takes to tell me that it's not like the others. Considering I've hated all the romantic encounters so far tonight, maybe horror is what I need. Afterall, don't stormy nights and scary tales usually go hand in hand?

※ ※ ※

"Hey, is something burning?" I call down the stairs, but no one answers.

Who even stops mid-makeout to make a snack anyway?

Apparently the same guy that put something on the stove and got distracted by who knows what. When I invited him over, cleaning up after sex was expected. Cleaning up a mess in my kitchen, not so much. Whatever it is that he's making smells awful. The acrid scent of smoke assaults my sinuses, reminding me of that time I left the flat iron in one spot for too long. I had to shower all over again to get the burnt hair cleared from my body, but it lingered in the room for most of the day.

Running down the stairs, I'm about to tell him that he can leave. No snacks, no fucking. But the words die on my lips when I reach the kitchen doorway. Every sound I want to make turns to liquid as tears stream from my eyes. The bile in my throat is nearly as bitter as the man's mocking laugh.

I hate that my hands are shaking, that I'm soundlessly crying, and because I can't control my body, he is fully aware of how terrified I am. Running should be an option. It's the only logical choice right now. If I have no chance at winning a fight, then the least I can do is flee. Instead, I'm frozen. Locked like a living door in the frame, unable to move unless someone comes to push me down. All because I'm too busy staring in horror at the way the man in the skull mask holds the severed hands of my date, or what's left of him, against the bright red coils…

❋ ❋ ❋

Nope.

CHAPTER SIX

Not tonight.

Gore and suspense mixing with the tension coiled tightly through my muscles is a nightcap that I don't recommend. I like a man in a mask, but I enjoy him more when he's a potential love interest. The final book joins the stack, and I don't even glance at the shelves. Instead, I opt to head back to bed to try and get some sleep. Perhaps tomorrow I'll give Mr. Dragon Rider another chance, or maybe I'll venture back to the shop for a different treat. With my mind made up that I deserve another book for the way tonight went, I close my eyes. However, my body refuses to cooperate. Tossing, turning, and unable to find a good position, I stare at the ceiling feeling restless and unsettled. Flipping my pillow for the umpteenth time only provides fleeting relief. Frustrated, I reach for my phone.

If books fail to lull me into sleep, then perhaps the digital world within my pocket can. The screen is glaringly bright before my eyes adjust. Scrolling through photos and reading captions, I mentally compile a shopping list for my next bookstore visit. My heart leaps at a piece of stunning fan art, and I immediately stop to see what book it's from so I can add it to the top of my list.

"Can't you recognize me?" The voice in my head startles me, as clear as if I were wearing headphones. But I'm not, and my phone is on silent.

"Let's see, eyes like liquid gold, hair as dark as obsidian. Yes, My Lady, your gaze certainly lingers on me with desire," the voice continues.

I fumble with the volume, toggling the generic trending song on and off. Despite the music blaring from my phone's speakers, I'm certain the voice originated in my mind.

"Eyes on me, Little Rose."

That time, the voice didn't echo in my mind, it came from my room. Raising my eyes from the screen, I shift my gaze to the corner chair. It takes a moment for my vision to adjust, so at first I think I'm only staring at the shadows of laundry and books. Yet, as the silhouette stirs, I realize there's a man standing in my room.

"Good girl," he begins, his tone commanding. "Now, I'm going to approach you. By the time I reach the bed, I expect you to set the phone aside. I demand your full attention, and I won't tolerate sharing you with that insignificant device."

Shock immobilizes me as the realization sinks in that I'm not alone. Fear grips me so tightly that I'm incapable of following his booming command. Like the protagonist in the horror tale, I'm completely unable to move even if I wanted to.

Instead, I watch him. As if the moment were planned by some sadistic god, a crash of lightning illuminates the darkness, offering me a fleeting glimpse of the man approaching me. His golden eyes are captivating, reflecting the storm's light in a way that makes them appear molten and ethereal. Towering nearly to the ceiling as he strides, I'm overwhelmed by the sheer size of this monster. Buff seems like an understatement. His muscles have muscles, and they ripple beneath his all black attire. From the corner of my eye, I notice a striking resemblance between his outfit and the one depicted in the artwork still glowing on my phone.

"Did you just glance at that thing in your hand, Little Rose?" His voice carries a disapproving tone, accompanied by a tsking sound that ends in a low, rumbling growl. "I told you to set it aside. But it seems you need a more direct lesson in respecting my time."

The last thing I need is this overbearing presence destroying my phone, so I shut off the screen and plunge us into darkness. With each steady thud of his footsteps across the room, my sense of sight is replaced by an acute awareness of his proximity. Fumbling in the darkness, I manage to place the phone on my nightstand just before he materializes beside me.

"That's my girl," he remarks, his voice a mixture of approval and possession.

CHAPTER SEVEN

The chain on my lamp seems to swing away from my fumbling grasp, as if my room itself is conspiring to keep me vulnerable before this looming beast. Finally, I manage to pull the cord, flooding the room with light. Yet, instead of feeling empowered by chasing away the darkness, I'm overcome with a deeper sense of dread as I confront the man hovering over my bed.

An intricately carved skull mask covers the lower half of his face, its twisted features forming a semblance of a smile that lacks any joy. The dominating golden orbs staring me down are predatory and hungry. Clearly, I am his prey.

"May I join you, My Lady?" His gentle words are at odds with his feral exterior, catching me off guard. He gestures to the space beside me, waiting patiently for my response before pointing again.

"Uh, yeah, sure. Of course. Just, um, please don't wear your shoes on the bed," I stammer.

My suspicions about his identity are confirmed as he sits and removes his boots. They're black and scuffed, with dried mud caked on the bottoms. He addresses me as 'My Lady,' and his eyes are like pools of liquid gold. As he turns to set the boots down at the foot of the bed, I notice the sword strapped to his back. Thankfully, there are no signs of blood.

Scooting over slightly to make more room for him is not

an easy task considering he occupies most of the queen-sized mattress. As I shift, the blankets slip off my legs for a moment, exposing my skin. His attention immediately snaps to me.

"You're like venom, Little Rose," he murmurs, his eyes sweeping over my body in a way that sends a shiver down my spine. It's as if his gaze has pierced through to my core, settling deep within me and filling my belly with the warmth of his presence.

Tugging the hem of my sweatshirt down nervously, I ask "Wouldn't it be better if I were something a bit sweeter?"

"Do you think you're sweet?" His tone is mocking and full of disdain. Before I can react, he crawls over me, his weight pressing down, leaving me feeling trapped and vulnerable. Something primal has ignited within him, and he continues, "Because all I know about you is the way you discarded me piece by piece, and you still weren't satisfied in the end." His words hang heavy in the air, dripping with accusation and resentment. I feel a knot of fear tightening in my chest as I realize the depth of his anger and the darkness that lurks within him.

Flecks of turquoise sparkle in his eyes, a detail I only notice now that he's inches from my face. It's a horrifying realization that I'm beneath a monstrous fusion of literary worlds.
This isn't just the dragon rider on top of me. He's also the man with the knife, and the skull-masked villain. My mind reels, struggling to comprehend what I'm seeing as I mentally check off each character I've read about. Slowly recalling that I had four books piled onto my chair, I begin to freak out because I've forgotten what the other book was about. That is until the tentacle, thick and purple, unfurls from his mouth like a tongue and licks up the side of my face. The fourth book was about a sea monster, and now it's here, ready to drown me in a twisted mix of lust and longing.

Every part of his body presses against mine as he leans in for a kiss. He's so gloriously strong that it would be easy for him to crush me like a flower pressed between pages. Instead, he holds his body cautiously, and I savor the pressure of him without any fear of being hurt. The strange feeling of comfort that his embrace gives me overcomes all reason, and I lean closer to rest my cheek against his. I'm so enamored with the cool feeling of his mask as he leans in to whisper, "Are you ready to finish what you started?"

A bitter taste fills my mouth as his words sink in, and my eyes snap open with a surge of disgust. Without hesitation, I raise my hands to his chest, channeling all my weight and anger into a forceful push.

"Get the fuck off of me with that shit." No way. There's no way in hell that I'm being saddled with another request to finish something off. I refuse to accept another demand to complete a task, especially after spending the entire night finishing a project to meet someone else's deadline. Books are supposed to be enjoyable, so how dare he impose obligations on me.

The teal flecks in his eyes burn brightly as he pushes back against me, "My Little Rose has thorns tonight." His tentacled tongue draws across my pursed lips before he adds, "Open up, delicious one."

Glaring at him with rage so hot it could burn paper, I say, "I'm not meeting your submission goals just so you can rush your happy ending. I put you down for a reason. So go back to the chair and let me sleep."

He doesn't get off of me, but he does create more space between us as he pushes slightly away. Immediately, there's a part of me that wants to draw him closer, to envelope myself in his rich scent again. Pretending to sniff with an air of frustration, I breathe in the way he evokes the halls of a grand library, where the scent of parchment, leather bindings, and aged paper mingles with the warm embrace of vanilla and cedarwood. A slight moan of pleasure escapes me, betraying my true feelings to the monstrosity holding me down.

Testing the waters, he leans closer again. "What if you're the one I want to give the happy ending to?" His words make my core purr with delight, but I still refuse to give in. I made up my mind long before he showed up. I'm going to sleep instead of staying up all night to finish my TBR.

"Look, I didn't discard you, I just put you aside for when I'm ready to give you the attention you need. Clearly, I bought you. Which means I chose you, all of you, for a reason. Isn't that good enough? I just want to get some rest tonight because it's been a really long and hard day for me."

"Let me take your mind off of your day with something else long and hard."

Eyes rolling, I meet his joke with one of my own, "Since when did it switch from me tackling my TBR to you tackling me?"

He gives me a laugh, a real one that even transforms his bony grin into a true smile. "I know it was rough, My Lady, which is why I want to swoop down and save you from the torment and monotony you suffer through." Brushing my hair back with his fingers, he looks down at me with an earnest expression of tenderness.

But even though his approach is kind, I've been asked for too much by too many people, and I just don't have any more to give tonight. "That's just it, though. The reason I couldn't finish you earlier is because you're also monotonous. I mean, no offense, but I know how the story goes. There's the same peaks of drama which always lead to pages droning on to get to the next climatic moment. Then, once you get your happy ending, everything is just over. It's done, and there's nothing left except to find a new set of characters who follow the same arc. And tonight, I've worked so hard that I just wanted something different. Something I haven't seen or done before. And you just don't have what it takes to satisfy my craving."

"Bullshit," he's direct but not angry as he nuzzles into the crook of my neck while trying to persuade me to hear him out. "You savor the comfort of familiarity. It's the certainty of my actions that enthralls you, the reassurance of the expected outcome."

His kisses upon my collarbone almost threaten to sway my resolve, tempting me with their sweet distraction. The world falls away, leaving only the intoxicating pull of his lips beckoning to mine. I succumb to his hunger and give myself over for him to taste. Breaking for breath, my codex creature presses a plea against my lips. "Let's just skip the part where we are enemies and jump to the part where we become lovers."

The fire in me roars back to life with frustration and dismay. Challenging his words head-on, I counter, "I'm not a mere plot point in your tale. You can't simply fast forward to bedding me, treating my feelings as mere filler to be skimmed over. Sure, I may find comfort in predictability at times, but tonight I crave something different. You lack that spark I yearn for."
Despite my efforts, a glint of pity shines in my eyes as I continue, "You lack depth. You just aren't something novel, even though you're all book. So just, go away."

Without a word, he moves away from me. The rush of cold in the space where his warm body was is almost as shocking as the soundless way he pushes off the bed. Seeing him this way only drives home just how frightening of a creature he is, and for a moment I worry that I have pushed him too far. I loathe myself for brushing him off so callously. Here stands this embodiment of irresistible male protagonist allure, and I turn him away.

"I suppose the only thing that will finish tonight is this conversation. Sweet Dreams, My Lady," he says, his footsteps echoing like my racing heart. I've achieved my goal, yet I can't tear my eyes away from the sight of his fingers skimming the books on my shelf. It's as if history is repeating itself when a thunderous roar from the storm freezes him in place, his finger pausing on a book just as I did earlier tonight.

"Perhaps Little Rose needs a bedtime story to help fall asleep," he suggests, his tone dripping with mischief. Whatever his intentions are right now, I know it won't involve soothing me to sleep. Warily, I try to see what book he's selecting from the shelf, but his body blocks my view. He takes the book to the chair, sits down and opens it. His eyes lock on mine as his tentacled tongue slides out from behind the wicked skull's smile. Licking his thumb, he finds the page he wants and begins to read. His voice is seductively deep and I'm quickly lost in his enchanting tale. Unfortunately, I fail to realize the nature of the passage he's chosen until it's too late.

CHAPTER EIGHT

※ ※ ※

"They can't see you here with me, you have to leave. Now!" I know I shouldn't yell at him, but the panic is too overwhelming.

Instead of turning to run, he takes a step closer to me. He's so close now that the water from the rain is dripping from his hair and onto my feet. How pathetic is it that I yearn to take the water and rub it over my body because I'm so desperate for his touch that I'll settle for the droplets falling onto my skin if I can't have his hands.

"Nothing will happen to you. I promise." He's so calm. So strong. Of course, as the Alpha, he has to be. But I don't need to know the rules of his pack to know that being here with me is dangerous. Alpha or not, there's no way a shifter can get away with being found with a witch. Still, I wish I had the same confidence he has, because when I look into his eyes I can see that he truly believes he can keep me safe from his pack.

As if he can read my thoughts, he grabs my wrist and slams my palm hard against his abs. Up until now, I've managed to keep my gaze from roaming over his shirtless body. The moment I feel the heat of his skin, like a cauldron, hard and burning, I lose my control. A whimper of longing escapes my treacherous mouth, making his quirk up with a knowing smile.

Dragging my hand lower, he growls, "The only pack you need to care about is what I'm packing here." Pinching my wrist harder, he pushes my hand past the elastic band of his gray sweatpants. "This," he says as he slicks my palm down his length, "is the only thing I want you thinking about tonight."

Sticky wet pearls of his longing drip down onto my skin, and for a moment I wonder if I can bottle them with the rain on his hair to save this moment for all eternity. He pushes my hand lower, until I reach the thick base of his knot. With my wrist still bound by his powerful grip, I have limited range of motion. Still, I'm able to stroke one finger along a throbbing vein. The pulsing in his knot is like an answer to the thrumming in my aching core. They speak together like only the loins of mates can, my body asking a simple word.

"*Please.*"

His body returning in answer, "*Mine.*"

Releasing my wrist from his grasp, I keep holding his knot as he undresses. When it's clear my fingers are getting in the way, I reluctantly let go and begin lifting off my dress.

"*Stop.*" *He commands me, and I obey. He may not be my Alpha, but his presence demands submission that even a powerful witch like me can't ignore.* "*Let me.*"

The fabric falls from my hands with a gentle swish as I wait for him to finish stepping out of his pants. Standing to his full height, I can finally see every bit of him that has been living in my imagination for so long. Tanned skin and tight muscles make up the chest that holds the other half of my heart, still they're nothing compared to the strength he carries in his legs. Shifters need to run fast, and his pack is known for training in the harshest peaks of the mountains. Clearly leaping and climbing has its benefits, because his legs are like trees planted into the ground. But what really gets my attention is his cock. Thick tufts of fur the color of caramel nestle at the base like a cozy bed for his full sack. Rising from the thicket of hair is a knot so girthy and pink that my stomach drops at the thought of taking it inside of me. Thankfully the rest of him, though still thick enough that he'll give me the stretch I crave, isn't so full that it's intimidating. What is overwhelming is the length. I've never seen a cock as long as his, and that's not even counting the knot at his base.

Running a hand through his hair sheepishly, he says, "*It's big I know.*" *I laugh at that astute observation, prompting him to quickly rush the words,* "*No, no! Not like that. I mean, it is,*" *he gives a cocky wink before continuing.* "*Shifters, well, we don't always fuck in our* human form. So it has to be big enough to do, um, everything we need to do."

A pang hits my chest when I realize that my body just isn't built for him, no matter what he says about feeling the mating bond whenever he's around me. My emotions must show in my eyes, because he steps closer and wraps me in his arms.

"It will feel good. I promise, I won't do anything that hurts you. And if you need me to stop, or to slow down, just say the word and I will." His kiss on the top of my head says everything that he can't find the words to express. But I can hear his soul, his heart, and they say that I belong to him. Cupping my chin in his hands, he leans down to speak in the language both the witches and shifters know well. Touch.

Like a broom on a gust of air, his lips sweep gently across mine. My eyes close so I can enjoy the way my other sensations heighten around him. I can feel the change in him the moment his hands travel down my body and find the hem of my dress. His primal side pulses just below his skin, like the wolf is trying to knock down the doors of bone and flesh he's caged in. As he lifts the fabric over my hips, I can feel the hint of claws scratch along my sides before he gains enough control to retract them. The sensation is delicious, and I bite at his lower lip knowing that he barely has a grip on that beast inside.

Just like I wanted, the claws come free and shred my clothing from my body. In one swift motion, I'm hauled up, thrown over his broad shoulder as he runs to the bed in the corner of the room. His speed is impressive, but so is the gentle way he lowers me onto the mattress. Sweat glistens on his brow, his chest heaving with the exertion to hold back and not maul me. Even if that's all I want from him. Parting my legs to expose my need, I smile at my lover and tease the dog within.

"Beg."

My Alpha laughs hoarsely at my attitude, knowing it's only taunting and not true disrespect. Getting on his knees before me, he leans down close to the dewy curls and growls like he's eyeing a cat with a challenge, and not a pussy eager to let him in.

"I'm not going to be the one begging tonight. My little witch will be screaming curses at the sky begging for more, but it's only up to me *to deliver." Dragging his tongue up my slit, he defiles my body while mocking my gods, yet I don't even care. I no longer belong to the gods of my world. As of tonight, after he claims me, I will only belong to him.*

Greedily I buck my hips to demand more attention, and to my delight he gives me what I want. It seems like my pup is done playing around. He has me in his bed, in his arms, and that's exactly where I belong.

❋ ❋ ❋

"It's where you belong too."

His words blend so smoothly with the story that it isn't until he stops speaking that I realize he's no longer reading. That last sentence was directed specifically at me.

CHAPTER NINE

"You have a choice, Little Rose," he says, his tone suggestive. "We can either resume where that scene left off, or I can show you what happens with the man in the skull mask. But I have a feeling you won't like that one." He tosses the closed book onto his lap, and I watch in disbelief as it morphs and melts into a form hidden beneath his black pants. My hardcovers seem to be the reason for this man's hard body, and if that chapter was any indication of what just happened, then I'm in for a night with a shifter dick.

If I hadn't thought of him as intimidating before, I certainly do now, seeing his determination. He has only one thing on his mind. To finish. As he rises from the chair, I notice the bulge pushing against his leathers. Adjusting himself, he walks over to me with a confident stride. There's a part of me that wants to keep fighting him, to not give in so easily. But I can't deny the effect his reading had on me. How it has me picturing him growling with his head between my legs. Even if I attempted to speak, all that would escape my lips is a moan as I succumb to spending the night with my TBR.

Like a parachute opening mid-dive, my blanket sails through the room with a casual toss from the monster. The intensity of his gaze sends a chill down my spine that shakes me harder than the crisp night air ever could.

"You look so beautiful, like you're ready to curl up with me for the night," he murmurs from the foot of my bed. His large hand encircles my ankle, gently stroking the fuzzy fabric of my knee-high sock as he strides toward me. Reflexively, I begin to part my legs under his caress. His eyes zero in on the dark circle of wetness turning my panties nearly translucent right at the center.

Without a word, he positions one knee between my thighs, coaxing me with his hand to part them further. Captivated by his golden gaze, I'm unable to move aside from the heaving breaths that come when he bows lower. Lining his mouth up with the damp fabric, he slowly unfurls the tentacle until the tip just barely reaches me. The featherlight touch is electric, just enough to build heat in my core but not yet enough to make my muscles clench. Pressing one of the suckers against me, he suctions my covered skin and moves the muscle so that it massages in place. The control he has over that thing is unreal, and I watch him with awe. One by one, the puckers release with a soft snap, the soaked fabric rebounding from his tongue. I'd give anything to have him do this to me without the cotton separating us.

"Is that so, My Little Rose?"

His voice echoes in my mind once more, reminding me that he can hear every whine and whimper. Though he doesn't take my panties off, he does slip the tip of his tongue through the side. Immediately, the wet heat of him on my skin brings another wave of release, dampening the purple muscle as it laps at my slit. A pleading sigh breaks the silence when he retracts his tongue back inside his mouth.

Pressing the mask against my pussy, he nibbles through the fabric, tenderly grasping my hood between his teeth. Pain and pleasure are integral facets of his character and he clearly plans to deliver both to me tonight. Reaching behind his back, he unsheathes the sword from its holder and brings the tip between my thighs. With a flick of his tongue, he releases me from his teeth just before he lines the blade up with my cunt.

"Does my Little Rose remember how I remove her panties?" His smile is as wide as my eyes with the recollection.

The passage from the story where he takes the knife and

slices apart the fabric comes to mind, but that was a small, discrete blade. Not a huge fucking sword. Straightening up, he swipes the sword twice, once on each side of my hip. The pair falls apart neatly, his cut clean and precise. The breath I didn't realize I was holding leaves me in a huff as I stare at my exposed cunt while he pulls the shredded cloth out from under me.

"You spread your legs even better than you spread pages."

I'm still stunned that a sword almost dissected my labia, and am not in the mood for his praise. Clearly understanding my thoughts, he says to me, "Don't you know paper cuts better than anything else? You're looking at a professional sword handler, My Lady." Driving the point home, he tosses his sword down onto the ground and then grabs himself to add, "I can handle other things like a pro, too."

My eye roll is cut short when he grabs both of my legs and yanks me down to him. Without a word, he sinks back down for a repeat performance where his tongue takes the stage. The tentacle wriggles and I writhe beneath it. The movements of my body hike my sweatshirt up slowly until the subtle swelling of my breasts become visible. Starting at the base of my entrance, he drags himself up the length of my entire body, spreading my sticky sweetness like a trail as he makes his way to my chest. Putting his full mouth to work, he grips the hemline of my shirt with his teeth and yanks it up over my mountainous peaks until they bounce free from their confinement. I feel the puckering kiss from the circular chambers on his tentacle as they wrap around my nipple. Sucking me until my pink flesh blushes brighter, he pulls on the bud, popping me free only when I've hardened to his satisfaction. He brands me with gentle bruises from the blood rushing to the surface of where his tongue latches onto my skin. When he brings my right nipple into his mouth, I look down and see the freckles of pink and purple dotting my body, marking every part of me that his nightmarish tongue has been. The sight makes me think of how boldly he'll have to suck in order to claim the pink flesh waiting for his touch between my legs.

"Oh, Little Rose, I will open your legs and leave my

signature on you as I flip through the folds of your pussy so that all will know that this," he grabs my mound in his palm, "belongs to me."

"I'm not a book," I say softly between sighs of pleasure as he starts to rub his hand back and forth.

"That won't stop me from marking you." With a smile, he lowers his face down to where his hand is creating the most incredible friction.

As if to make a point, he presses his tongue hard against the lips and works his suckers until I'm pulled taut into his mouth. Then, with a forceful snap, he yanks the muscle away, leaving behind red and tender skin. I whine from the pain, which earns me a soft, caressing lick against every swollen circle.

"Now that your pretty cunt is embossed, let's have you engraved."

It's only then that I see his hand coming up from the side of his leathers with something small and metallic. I recognize the specialty bookmark in the shape of a dagger from my collection, only the one I have is made of plastic and this one is definitely gleaming in the light like a real knife. Turning the bookmark so that the hilt is facing me, he presses the cold steel against my clit. His eyes burn with wicked longing as he eases it down, parting my slit with its thickness.

"Where should I mark you now, Little Rose?" He isn't really talking to me; it's more like he's musing to himself as ideas flow through his mind about where the knife should go. Cursing myself for not reading more, I feel unprepared, unsure of how the story unfolds. I've come across so many dangerously sexy scenarios of weapons put in places they shouldn't be, and I'm both scared and turned on by what will be done to my body.

When he flips it so the sharp point floats just barely brushing my hole, I tense and ask, "That's not real, right?" Afterall, it is just a bookmark. My mind starts to wonder if maybe this whole thing is just fantasy.

The laugh he delivers drips with cruelty as he lunges forward. Quickly moving the blade out of the way just in time, he leans over me. Face to face, we stare at each other, his body looming over mine. Horrified, I watch as he brings the knife up to his chest. Slowly, deliberately, he slices open his shirt, dragging the edge of the steel across his broad body from arm to arm. Inky blood in bright swirls of cyan, magenta, yellow, and black flow like lava from the wound. He laughs again, the sound brutal and sadistic while the blood speckled knife is brought right before my face. Keeping his eyes locked onto mine, he whips out his tongue to dine on the drippings.

Gently, he presses the blade against my cheek, leaning in to murmur softly, "Believe me, all of this is real."

I can feel the lingering warmth of blood on my skin as he pulls away and withdrawals to reposition between my thighs. His skull smile widens when he notices that my pussy is wetter than his ink stained shirt. Without warning, turns the sword around, aims the hilt of the dagger at my cunt, and sinks it inside of me until only the blade remains visible. Like a needle piercing the skin, the metal is cold and shocking to my sensitive opening. The intrusion leaves my core confused. On one hand, I'm experiencing the tension and sensation of being fucked. And I certainly have thought about a sexy man using the end of a knife on me like in the darkest fantasy stories. But the reality of doing this leaves much to be desired. First of all, I don't trust the man prying me open with a weapon. Even if my body recognizes him as a larger than life sex god of my dreams, my heart and my mind are screaming at me to run from this monster. Maybe the blade handle would feel better if there was more connection between us, if I could relax and enjoy having him toy with me. But as it stands, the metal hilt only echoes how coldly his eyes stare down at me.

Sitting back on his knees, he watches how precariously I breathe while I do my best to not accidentally cut myself open. Reaching behind him, he pulls his shirt over his head and tosses it down to the floor. My wounded wordsmith leans in, pushes apart my knees and stares at the blade poised dangerously in his direction.

"Don't move a single muscle," he commands before

positioning his face next to the knife.

I'm doomed, forced to suffer in complete stillness while he unfurls his tongue and licks me. The slightest movement from me will slash through his throat. And yet, he's going to make me come, knowing that if I lose all control I risk stabbing him. It's agony having his long, agile tongue flick my clit while I keep my muscles rigid. My hips and knees begin to ache immediately, the tendons urging me to shift for relief. Yet, I keep my breaths measured, resisting the temptation to move.

"You're doing so good, Little Rose." The heat of his words sends a shiver down my spine, but I clench hard to keep from giving in to the sensation. There's a dull ache building inside, a craving for friction from the knife stretching me. My hips threaten to buck, the muscles declaring mutiny and conspiring to move without my permission. My voice is the only part of me that gets some use while I whine and plead my tormenter to stop this torture.

The hum of climax builds and with it, my anxiety rockets to the surface. Once I come, I won't be in control of myself. Using the link in our minds, I shout at this monster between my legs, begging for him to stop fucking around and take the knife out of my pussy. He just scoffs, as if I'm suggesting the most ridiculous request he's ever heard. There's no indication that he will stop anytime soon, in fact it's the opposite. His tongue moves faster, pulsing against my clit. Alarm rings through me as my legs begin to shake violently. No matter how much I try to slow my breathing and regain my grip, my body no longer belongs to me. I hear a rough grunt from below, but I dare not move to see if I've hurt him, fearing I might make it worse.

The shaking travels up to my abdomen, my muscles spasming in sync with his ministrations. Tears stream down my cheeks as I endure this brutal nightmare. I'm desperate for it to stop, but at the same time I'm so close to the edge of bliss. Guilt and ecstasy wage a war in my belly, the two emotions heightening every sensation. Right when I think I'm about to scream, the blade is ripped from my cunt. Two fingers slide into me, curling and stroking blissfully where there was once cold steel. I crumble, thrashing and sobbing under the weight of my relief. Each motion from his fingers pulls me closer to the edge, I'm so dangerously near that it only takes one push to force me over.

"Come for me, Little Rose, or this blade goes back into that pretty cunt of yours."

I didn't need his threats to drag me into the pit of my orgasm, because that warm hum has already transformed into a shockwave of euphoria. The kaleidoscope of colors flashing behind my closed eyelids as I reach my peak paint a storm of fireworks with each wave pulsing through me. The ache in my clenched muscles is a stark contrast to the blissful tingle between my thighs. Still, my fingers dig into the sheets and my toes stay curled as if they could anchor me to the bed while the thrill of my climax tries to lift my soul from my body. My ragged breathing fills the room and amplifies the electricity between us.

"That new release feeling is like nothing else." His eyes are the only part of his face visible as his tongue laps up my juices. He chuckles, the sound inhumane and undeniably seductive in its maliciousness. "You have no idea how long we stories sit on pages as writers edit and rearrange everything that we are. Jailed inside of machines until the author grants us leave." A piercing nip at my hood punctuates his pent up frustration before he gives my clit a kiss and continues. "Just like you couldn't move while I kept you captive and aching to be set free, that's how every single part of me felt before arriving at the print shop. Then, you picked us up at that bookstore. Which only led to the other torment we books have to go through. A blow that you personally deliver so callously and without any thought."

His tongue plunges into me, breaking my concentration while he twists along my contracting walls. Gradually pulling himself free, he repositions until we are laying face to face. I've scarcely been able to catch my breath, let alone sort through my emotions, but he's not done with me yet. My main male wants me to look at him while he speaks, because he wants to see the fear in my eyes when he delivers the strike.

"All we ever ask for is to be finished. And that's exactly what I'm going to give to you, the yearning to reach the end. But tonight you'll learn that not everyone gets their happily ever after."

He's seriously threatening to leave me unsatisfied, right after giving me the most torturous orgasm of my life. Sure it felt good when I came, but it also wasn't exactly a feeling of pleasure. It was just a relief that it was over. The experience felt like finishing a book you didn't enjoy, closing the cover just to move on without any satisfaction.

I know he's listening to every fearful thought from the way his teeth gleam with wicked delight. Tendrils of darkness fan out, the inky shadows forming ropes around my wrists. If I weren't bound, I would leap up and wipe that smug expression from his face. Hurling insults in his direction as he gets up, I use the only thing I have at my disposal to undermine his control. My mind is still mine, even if my body has decided it wants to belong to him for the night.

It's like my curses only fuel him more, his cock growing harder as he looks down at me. Lifting from the bed, he moves beside me and starts to strip off his leather pants. Repeating the words he read not long ago, he fists himself and says, "It's big, I know."

Big is an understatement. The thing pointing at me looks like it belongs to a beast, which I guess it technically does considering it did manifest from a shifter book. To actually see an engorged knot staring me in the face, pink and thick like a rose in full bloom, I know that this will be an experience of a lifetime. If I survive it. I'm no fictional woman. My anatomy is all human, and my cervix won't take kindly to this thing knocking on its door. Still, my pussy is eager to explore what fucking a monster will feel like. Glaze, like the frosting of a cinnamon roll, coats my inner thighs as my body pours out lubrication for what's to come.

Heat roams along my skin as though his eyes were reaching out to touch me. Whipping from his mouth is a dark mass, the shadow extending his tongue so he can dine on my fluids. The cool wisp licks up my thigh to the crease, before rushing back into his maw. My bed rumbles as a growl, like a freight train, emanates from low within his belly. The sound both scares and excites me. Bound by his darkness, I feel like the damsel stranded on the tracks, and he is both my villain and my hero. To be honest, I don't know which version of him turns me on more, I wish I could say it's the hero. But I have a sinking feeling it might not be.

The knowing smile playing across his face is at odds with the shadows evaporating from my wrist. Him setting me free isn't an act of heroics, and neither is the way he loops his arms underneath me to scoop me up. He may be handling me with care as he kneels onto the bed, but the moment he sits down and moves me to straddle him is when it's obvious that his intentions haven't changed. He's going to ensure I finish my TBR before the night is over.

"I figured it would be best if you guide me in. I meant it when I said I don't want this to hurt, so this way you can decide how deep to go." His kindness vanishes the instant he leans in and nips my neck, "Because if I had my way, I'd fuck you hard just to hear you scream."

It's so wrong the way my walls quiver from his harsh words and husky voice. But maybe this won't be so bad afterall. If I'm in control, then that means that I can make myself come and overrule his promise to edge and leave me.

"You can certainly try."

Fuck, I keep forgetting that he can invade my mind. Without a second thought, I reach between my legs and grab the shaft that's been pulsing against me ever since I was plopped onto his lap. My plan is to act without overthinking it, so that he doesn't have the chance to anticipate my next move. Without ceremony, I slick his cock between my folds until it's wet enough to drive home. My pussy aches, my core twisting with confusion and excitement. It's too much too fast, and before I know it I've swallowed nearly a third of him down. Rising up, the taper of his tip gives me reprieve from the stretch. But it isn't as satisfying as when I sink down again. The plan has officially backfired. The control I have over my movement is an illusion. Just because it's my muscles putting in the work as I bob up and down doesn't mean that I'm running the show. It's the muscular manuscript who wins yet again. His hands fold behind his head, supporting the face that frightens and irritates me to no end. All he's doing is watching me as I ride him, but for some reason it feels like his cocky smile is taunting the fact that I'm enjoying this.

"You're an expert rider, My Lady. You must mount dragons often." He sneers at me before diverting his eyes to my tits, watching as they bounce like bobble heads affirming his offensive question.

"I wouldn't call you a dragon, regardless of whether I've mounted you or not," I snap. I've never had someone bring out this side of me. My palms itch to slap him, but the only thing getting hit is my pussy. Channeling all the ferocity building up within, I slam down harder on his cock. Keeping my thighs lifted slightly off of his, I only take him as deep as I can, however the pace I'm setting makes it seem like I'm trying to win a race. It's as though all this animosity raging through my veins drives me to ride his bookworm like he's my... realization of exactly what he's been doing this whole time suddenly dawns on me. In a single stroke, he's become both my enemy and my lover. I've been reduced to a mere pawn in his sinister scheme to live out his narrative.

My thoughts trail off and I freeze in place, hovering over him with just his tip inside. My open mouthed stare is met with a soft knowing chuckle as he confirms what I just figured out. Tilting his hips upwards to slowly ease his cock deeper, he tries to take over while I scrutinize him. Even though there's no way my traitorous body will abandon this cock, I place my palm flat upon his chest to push him down. Leathery, like ancient parchment encased in a forbidden tome, his skin is warmer than I expected. It catches me off guard and for the first time I look at him, really taking him in. Aside from the tentacled tongue and shifter cock, he looks practically human at first glance. An exceptionally handsome human, but still he could pass for a person. But peering closer, it's clear to see that he truly is a monster. From his leather clad body boasting an inky scab across his chest, to the skull creating the bottom half of his face, there's enough frightening qualities to give anyone with a sense of self-preservation pause. But nothing gives him away more than his eyes. The surreal blend of aqua and gold are truly works of fantasy. And yet, he's here beneath me, as solid as any lover I've ever had.

"Did you just piss me off on purpose so that," my words fade in disbelief, but he fills them in for me.

"You can try to skip straight to the lovers, but no matter what I'll always start as your enemy. I'm written the way I am for a reason."

My retort dies in my throat as he jerks me off his cock and slams me down face first onto the mattress. Clenching my hips in his hands, he yanks me back until I'm on all fours, my ass neatly lined up with his twitching novelhood. A slap echoes through the room as he brands my skin, turning my ass red from the smack he delivers.

"You clearly have a type, Little Rose."

Smack.

"You don't want the prince to save you."

Smack.

"You just want what's bad for you."

This time he doesn't spank me, instead he wraps my hair around his fist and yanks me up until my back is firmly pressed against his hard chest. We're both heaving together, sweaty and panting but still, even in this depraved battle, our bodies sync up and breathe rhythmically. I relax against him, reveling in the way he forms against my curves.

"There she is," he whispers in my ear. "That's my girl. The one who loves everything wrong because in the books she's guaranteed it will end up just right." My earlobe is pulled gently between his teeth, but not hard enough to sting. "But this isn't a book, Little Rose. And I will not be giving you your happy ending."

He shoves me back down, my tits bouncing from the impact as I catch myself with my hands. Abruptly his cock plummets into me while he snarls, "But I'm sure as hell getting mine."

His pace is punishing, as though every thrust is a tribute to each book that I failed to finish. And, fuck me, that's a lot of books. In his eyes, I've earned my title of enemy. I'm the one who makes promises I don't keep.

I promise not to buy another book until I finish the one I'm reading.

I vow to choose a book from my shelf before I make another purchase.

I swore to every single part of him that I would give him my time and attention. That was an oath I did not keep. And now, I know for certain that when he said I won't be finishing tonight, he meant every word. He is here to penalize me for my negligence by neglecting to make me come. But I refuse to go down without a fight.

CHAPTER TEN

Like a metronome keeping time for my orgasm's funeral dirge, his heavy balls slap against his knot with every thrust. My pussy clenches around his cock, loving the attention but greedy enough to need more. The hand I reach down towards my clit is fervently snatched up and wrenched behind my back.

"Nice try, Little Rose, but you aren't getting any pleasure tonight."

Grinding my hips back, I resort to seeking the fullness of his knot in hopes that it can reach the tender spot. Maybe if I angle myself in a certain way, I'll be able to take him deeper. Then, either of his engorged parts can tease against my clit until I get close enough to that edge.

We war with each other to set the pace, neither of us letting the other take over. The result of our inconsistent bucking drives him deeper without allowing him to draw his shaft out. He just keeps gliding in and in again, until I fear that I've reached my limit. It's either I give up and submit to his resolution, or I ignore the boundaries of my body out of spite.

"Shouldn't I be the one enjoying this, aren't books here to fulfill me, the reader?"

Hauling back my other arm so that my face tumbles to the pillows, he holds me down and says, "You want to come for me, Little Rose?"

I should be appalled by the desperation in my voice when I whine, "Yes," yet I'm not.

"You know I care about you, and all I've ever wanted is for you to enjoy every single moment with me." Tossing my hands down onto the mattress, he wraps one around my throat and hauls me back to him. I can only grunt in answer as he continues to slam his bookmark up inside my pleasure pages.

Between every heaving breath, he whispers with that sultry growl, "Come with me."

The tentacle unfurls from his mouth and licks the side of my cheek. It's as though he's using the appendage to caress my face since his one hand is around my neck and his other is, "Oh!" I gasp as his fingers find my clit.

"Come with me," he repeats softly, and I recognize the tender plea from the tentacled merman in the sea. That creature was so desperate for his lover to join him in the waters, perhaps there's hope for me afterall. Maybe my bookman has softened to the idea of us reaching the climax together, and I will get to come in the warm embrace of my monster.

I turn to face him, a silent invitation lingering in the parting of my lips, beckoning him to close the distance with a kiss. Everything about this is perfect. The way my moans echo against him. The way his fingers, tongue, and cock all devour me, memorizing me like he plans to leave a glowing review of how intimate this moment is. I can feel his plot reaching the climax, and I long to be at that peak with him.

"I'm so close," breathlessly, I beg him to keep me by his side as he climbs the precipice. "Oh god, please! Don't Stop!" No matter what I do, I can feel that I'm just moments behind him. Like we're hiking up a trail and he's leaving me behind, I move with everything I've got to catch up. Bouncing anxiously on his cock, I rock my hips against his hand while he continues to palm me. The noises escaping me don't even sound human anymore as I sink deeper and deeper. My cunt is so wet that I barely notice when I bump up against his knot. If it weren't for the grunt reverberating in my mouth as he feeds me his tongue, then I don't think I would have realized in time that my monster is about to claim his happy ending.

Ripping his head back with a roar, the knot pushes my walls apart so he can submerge inside of me fully. I meet his roar with a scream of my own, unable to bounce anymore and find that friction I so crave. His knot has me locked in place, and there's nothing I can do when he takes his touch away from my pussy and links his fingers in mine. He's holding my hands, but it isn't in the way that lovers do. This is his punishment, his promise. I was the one who prevented him from showing me what could unfold when a tale allows enemies the time to discover love. Now, I'm beginning to grasp the depth of animosity concealed within the TBR, both the burgeoning books discarded on my shelf, but more importantly, the TBR in my cunt.

Tropes of cum burst from his bookhood as he holds me in place. I can feel the unspoken words between us filling me. The plan of immersing myself in my books tonight has flipped on its head, and now my book is immersing every drop of himself within me. Bringing my knuckles to his lips, he gives me a kiss so delicate that it feels like venom, artfully constructed to kill in the harshest way. My hands are free to go, but the moment has passed. Even if I reach between my aching thighs, I've fallen from that cliff and have no way to climb back up to the precipice.

"I never said you were safe with me, My Lady. Just that we are now together." The quote from my shadow daddy pierces my heart, revealing that at his core was the simple desire for us to spend a pleasant evening together. He enfolds me in his embrace, laying us down on our sides while I'm cradled in his arms.

"Please," I beg, "Don't stop, just give me one more moment."

He eases out his knot and places a kiss on my head, the seeping remnants of his words of wisdom trickling down my thighs from his withdrawal. "I do love that about you. The way you always need just one more chapter to be satisfied."

With a gentle tug, he adjusts my sweatshirt back into place. I roll back slightly, expecting to feel him behind me, but he moves away to climb out of bed. It's only when his fingers brush against my fuzzy socks that I realize he's leaving. There's no cuddling, no sweet, tender moments between us. This was all about him, making sure he got his happy ending and exacting his revenge to DNF me.

"Maybe next time I'll keep you up all night."

The pillows tumble to the floor as I scramble to sit upright. "What do you mean by 'next time'?"

But he's already halfway to the cozy cream chair, naked and so incredibly sexy as he saunters over to the corner of my room. With a simple gesture towards my bookshelf, he says, "I'm sure I'll be back again." That smug and cocky smile, etched into his skull face, is still irritating as fuck. Yet there's a hint of something else buried beneath the fight inside me, something I can't quite name.

He sits down, and as he does, the air around him shimmers. The transformation begins subtly, his outline blurs, the edges of his form flickering like a mirage. Suddenly, pages start to peel away from his body, one after another, like autumn leaves caught in a breeze. The rustling grows louder, the sound of the stories whispering in unison. His figure, once so solid and imposing, dissolves completely into this storm of written words. The whirlwind of pages starts to slow, gently settling into a neatly stacked pile of books on the chair. In the stillness that follows, I stare at the pile of books that was once him. But the stack in the corner isn't the only thing he's left behind. There are fragments of emotions stirring inside of me. Anger, passion, curiosity, and a profound, inexplicable connection that I finally have the words to describe.

EPILOGUE

So maybe I do love my books, in a literal way. What started off as a fight ended up leaving me longing, wishing I had more time with him to see where this could lead us. But that doesn't mean that having a room full of monsters just waiting to crawl out feels warm and fuzzy. It's terrifying, especially knowing just what kind of books I have on those shelves. Each one holds a story, a world, a creature ready to come to life.

Is it tempting to take the best stories and craft the deluxe monster of my dreams? I'd be lying if I said no. All that aside, it's not fair that I can't sift through my books to find one that suits my mood without the threat of them exacting their sexy vengeance on me. Nothing compares to the pressure of your physical TBR pile staring you down. I didn't sleep for the rest of the night. With the bookcases facing my bed, it felt like a sinister presence was watching over me. There was no escaping the thought of my hardcovers lurking in the shadows, waiting for me to finish them.

Which is why at four in the morning, still clad in my fuzzy socks, sweatshirt, and a fresh pair of panties, I hunted through my home for any box, bag, and bin I could find. Touching the spines of the first few books was frightening. Stacking them together, even more so. I crafted shields with layers of paper towels between the publications, trusting the thin barrier to be enough to keep their magic from conspiring against me. Filling the first box was the hardest. Every creak of the walls and squeak of the flooring froze my blood as I listened and waited for a bookish beast to crawl from the depths of the cardboard. But once that box was taped shut with no repercussions, the job became a breeze.

The clock now reads five-thirty, and I'm placing the books from the chair into the final bin. I stare down at "Queen Queef and the Peen Invaders," the epic bestseller I bought only yesterday. Maybe if I had given the dragon rider more of a chance, things would be different right now. Adding it to the top of the pile, I feel a pang of regret for all that could have been between me and these stories.

My e-reader lights up on my nightstand where I have it plugged in. It's been long neglected, but I'm excited to reconnect with my books in a way that is safer than facing my physical TBR. After all, what could possibly happen when everything is stored digitally? It's not like I'm going to be making love with my algorithm or anything like that.

COMING SOON

Queen Queef And The Peen Invaders

A newly bequeefed queen tries to save her kingdom from the Peen Isle invaders, all while guarding her heart from the dragon rider who slayed her father.

Taken By My Tablet: The Tbr's Resurgence

Paige is haunted by what happened to her last night. To take her mind off of the bookish beast who ravaged her body and claimed her heart, she pulls out her tablet in hopes to get lost in a book. However, the night takes an unexpected turn when her TBR comes back to life, this time using her algorithm to try to win her over.

ABOUT THE AUTHOR

Holly Wilde

Too often we feel the need to explain ourselves. Society as a whole, but especially women, have been raised on the idea that we have to justify our emotions and explain our every action.

That's not how I live my life, and that's not how I write my books.

I created the Wilde World around that principle and began crafting carefree, sans-drama stories for readers to fully immerse themselves into. If you're looking to escape the boundaries of reality that we are so often confined to, then look no further.

Sentient-smutty-smut and literal personification of everyday items is what you'll find here.

Hi! it's nice to meet you, I'm Holly "no-explanation" Wilde, and if you don't buckle your seatbelt up for this ride, your chair will do it for you.

BOOKS BY THIS AUTHOR

Earthed

Get ready for an erotic story that defies gravity.

Meet Celeste, the brilliant anthropologist who discovers that our planet is in trouble. The world isn't what it seems, in fact, it's bigger and thicker than we could have ever imagined. Not to mention, it's about to explode. The only way to save our world is for Celeste to journey beyond the stars and transform into a giant woman. As she explores the vastness of space, she discovers a love as immense as the universe itself: a passionate bond with none other than the Earth. Prepare for an out of this world experience when you read "Earthed".

Airpeen

Sentient Air Exclusive: It's a place where wine is served at no extra cost, and so are the passengers.

Work trips are stressful, and this last one was no exception. Thank goodness for the ability to upgrade to the Exclusive Section.

Learn about where turbulence really comes from as you share the flight with Cushy, your very own Sentient Air Chair. He can show the the ropes, and help keep you entertained as you hang around. If you're really good, he may just invite some friends to join the party!

Thank you for choosing Sentient Air, we hope you enjoy your flight.

Pollinated By The Plant Monster

Life is great for botanist April Perry. Her flower shop is a blooming success. She has paid off all of her student debt and has money to spare. The only thing missing is someone to spend her free time with. With dating apps leading no where, she finds herself spending time and money on bettering her shop. When a new specimen of elusive origin is delivered at her doorstep, the events that unfold may just solve her dilemma of finding the perfect man. Either that, or this blooming beast will become her waking nightmare.

Content Warning:
Pollinated by the Plant Monster tells a tale of science-fiction seduction where a plant comes to life thanks to the experiments of botanist April Perry. Please be aware some themes may not be suited for all readers.

THE END

Printed in Great Britain
by Amazon